BOBBY BAINS PLAYS A
BLINDER

Lovely to meet you!

BALI RAI

illustrated by
Daniel Duncan

Barrington Stoke

Published by Barrington Stoke
An imprint of HarperCollins*Publishers*
Westerhill Road, Bishopbriggs, Glasgow, G64 2QT

www.barringtonstoke.co.uk

HarperCollins*Publishers*
Macken House, 39/40 Mayor Street Upper,
Dublin 1, DO1 C9W8, Ireland

First published in 2024

ISBN 978-1-80090-254-1

10 9 8 7 6 5 4 3 2 1

Printed and Bound in the UK using 100% Renewable Electricity
at Martins the Printers Ltd

MIX
Paper | Supporting
responsible forestry
FSC™ C007454

This book contains FSC™ certified paper and other controlled
sources to ensure responsible forest management.

For more information visit: www.harpercollins.co.uk/green

"Whatever kind of seed is sown in a field, prepared in due season, a plant of that same kind, marked with the peculiar qualities of the seed, springs up in it ..."

– Guru Nanak Dev-ji (Founder of Sikhism)

CONTENTS

1

FOOTBALL IS LIFE

I'd just played the perfect pass to a striker, and they'd scored a brilliant goal from it. My team-mates were mobbing me, and the massive crowd in the stadium were chanting my name. One hundred thousand people all shouted, "Bobby! Bobby!"

But then my teacher's voice broke into my daydream. "Bobby, do you know the answer?"

Mrs Richardson was teaching us Maths, and I don't really get Maths. It's like the numbers get all mixed up in my head. I have to focus really hard in order to understand, but just now I'd been away in a world of my own.

Next to me, Maisie and Bella giggled.

"Bobby was dreaming again," whispered Maisie.

"Weird," Bella replied.

"Not weird," said Maisie. "Just *boy*. They're a special kind of creature."

Mrs Richardson was not impressed.

"Maisie! Bella!" she warned. "Would you like to spend lunch-time on litter patrol?"

"No, Miss," Maisie replied.

"Then stop whispering and pay attention," Mrs Richardson told her.

She looked towards me and smiled. "Dreaming again, Bobby?" she asked.

"Yes, Miss," I said. "Sorry."

"Was it football again?" Mrs Richardson added.

"Er, yes, Miss," I told her. "Still sorry ..."

"There's more to life than football, Bobby," she said.

I love football – and I do mean *love*. I wake up thinking about it, and I think about it all day long. When I'm falling asleep, I dream about scoring the winning goal in a Champions League Final. Or the FA Cup. Or the Premier League. I don't care which competition – it's just a dream. The only thing that matters is the shirt I'm wearing. Liverpool FC.

My grandad loves football too, and he laughs at me when I tell him about my latest dreams of glory. But I don't call him "Grandad". I'm a Sikh, and my family speak both English and Punjabi. I call my grandad Nana-ji, because that's the

Punjabi word. Your grandad on your mother's side is your *nana*. And your grandad on your dad's side is your *baba*. Adding *ji* shows respect for them.

Sikh boys don't cut their hair, so mine is really long. My parents tie it up for me, into a bun. Then it's covered in fabric. The cover is called a *patka* – and I'm really proud of mine. It's a sign of courage and strength, and faith too. As an adult, Nana-ji has a turban and a beard, and he prays twice a day. But he says that when he was younger, he was less respectable – a troublemaker.

*

After school that day, Nana-ji came to me in my bedroom. He lives with me and Mum, which is another reason why we're really close. My dad left when I was a baby, so Nana-ji helps look after me.

"Bobby?" he called from the door.

"Come in, Nana-ji," I said.

He came and sat down on my bed. Nana-ji looked at my walls, which were covered in Liverpool FC posters. "Did I ever tell you about my first City game?" he asked.

I smiled and rolled my eyes. "Only five or six thousand times," I replied.

"You cheeky so-and-so!" he said, grinning at me.

Nana-ji is a massive City fan and was one of the first British Asian fans to attend City games. That was a long time ago, but he has lots of stories to tell, and he tells them a lot!

I pointed at the "Anfield Road" sign above my door. "But who cares about City?"

"Support your local team, son!" Nana-ji replied. "I should tell your mum off. She should never have let you go supporting Liverpool."

"City are OK, sometimes," I told him. "Mostly rubbish though."

Nana-ji poked my leg. "Leave it out, son," he warned, but I knew it was a joke.

"Did you play a lot of football when you were young, as well as watch City?" I asked.

"Yep!" he said excitedly. "Three times a week – for the school team, a Saturday League and a Sunday league, plus training. And we played in break-time at school every day. That was my life back then – football, reggae music, my mates ..."

"But you weren't a practising Sikh back then, were you?" I said to him.

"No, I wasn't," he replied. "I had long curly hair and was a rascal. I changed too."

"Why did you change?" I asked.

"I grew up," Nana-ji said. "Got married to your grandmother, had kids, bought a house.

Going out became less important. And I started to learn more about Sikhism."

"Do you miss her?" I asked.

"Your grandmother?" he said. "Every single day, Bobby. She was a good sort."

My grandmother died before I was born, but I've heard loads of stories about how lovely she was. I often feel sad that I didn't get to meet her.

"How come you don't play football now?" I asked. "Like, with other bald old men?"

Nana-ji grinned again.

"I can't run any more," he said, and his expression became glum.

"Sorry," I said, feeling guilty for making him sad.

Nana-ji shook his head. "It's OK," he told me. "Don't feel bad for asking. It's just one of those things, kid."

"I wish you could play again."

"Me too," he said. "But not with these old knees. Nowadays, I'm happy just to watch. And I still have my reggae music."

Reggae is Nana-ji's other big passion. He loves the music and has loads of old vinyl records, and cassettes too.

He said goodnight, hugged me and left.

I fell asleep dreaming of what my grandparents were like as youngsters. And football, of course. Always football …

2

A BIG WIN

My school is called Wigby Primary School, and I play for the football team. I also play for our local Saturday league team, Wigby FC Juniors, and we practise every Wednesday evening.

That Wednesday, I was freezing as I stood on the pitch, and my hands felt numb. We were doing a warm-up routine, but it wasn't making me any warmer.

"Time to get the footballs out!" said our coach, Byron.

We had five groups of three players. My group included my best friend, Thiágo, and another friend from school, Albie. Each of us had to dribble the ball between the cones, turn back and pass the ball on. Me and Thiágo were good, but Albie was amazing. The ball seemed to stick to his feet. He was the shortest player in the team, but he was fast and strong. People struggled to tackle him during games.

Once the drills were over, we played short five-a-side games, and the winners got to stay on. My group was always desperate to stay unbeaten. But this week, we only played three mini-games before we lost.

"You should have passed to me!" Thiágo told Albie.

"But I was sure I could score," Albie replied.

"Now we're going to get cold again," I said.

I began to jog on the spot and pulled my sleeves over my hands. Behind us, a group of adults stood chatting and watching. An older man, who looked about the age of Nana-ji, smiled as he watched. I wondered if he was the grandad of one of the other players.

After training, I went to meet Mum at the community centre she runs, which is next door to the park. The main hall had been lined with tables, ready for the regular weekly food bank. There was all sorts – tins of tomatoes and soup, and vegetables, toothpaste and toothbrushes, bread, flour, eggs. It was like a mini-supermarket, only everything was free.

Mum smiled when she saw me. "Come and join us," she said.

I walked over and dumped my bag under the table she was standing behind.

"You can help if you like," said Mum. "Or shall I take you home?"

"I'll stay," I told her. "I'm not tired."

I spent the next hour helping sort out the tins and packets of food. Just as we were about to close, the older man who had been watching us play football shuffled over. He was tall, with a grey beard and pale brown eyes. He looked lost and was frowning.

"Can I ...?" he said, pointing to the flour.

"Yeah," I said. "Please do."

He put a bag of flour into an old cloth bag. It had a logo on it that read "Two Tone Records" above black-and-white squares.

"You were watching the football earlier," I added.

The man glared at me. "So what?" he replied. "Free country, isn't it?"

He had a Caribbean accent.

"I'm sorry. I wasn't being rude," I told him. "Do you like football?"

His expression softened and his eyes lit up as if he'd remembered something awesome. "Yes," he said. "I used to love playing. More than anything in the world."

"I love it too," I told him. "I'm Bobby."

He nodded. "I'm Trevor," he replied.

"Do you still play football?" I asked.

He gave me a little smile. "No," he said. "Too old. I don't leave the house much now unless I have to."

"You could try playing football again?" I said without thinking. "My grandad used to play too. He loved it but says he can't run any more."

Trevor tapped his left knee.

"Same for me, kid," he replied. "You youngsters are lucky. Enjoy it while you can."

"I'm sorry," I said. "You must really miss it."

"I do," he said, before walking away.

I watched him go, wondering how old he was compared to Nana-ji and what position he played when he was younger.

"You OK?" Mum asked me.

"Getting tired," I said.

"I'll take you home," she replied. "Grab your stuff, kid."

★

That weekend, Wigby Juniors had a home game against Southfield Celts. They were our closest rivals. We had won more games than Southfield, but they started the game better. By half-time, we were 0–2 down, and Byron wasn't happy.

"You're not playing your own game," he told us. "You're not passing properly or focusing. Don't worry about what Southfield are doing. Stick to our game plan. Press their midfield and get the ball into the spaces on the wings. Come on, Wigby – you've got this!"

I lined up next to Thiágo for the kick-off. We're the same height, but Thiágo is thinner and faster than me. He has pale brown eyes and his hair is often braided. He speaks really softly, apart from when he plays football – then he is loud!

"Ready?" I asked.

"Yeah!" he replied.

We're both midfielders and had played badly in the first half. Now, we were determined to change things.

I looked across to Nana-ji and Thiágo's mum. They waved and smiled at us. Then I spotted Trevor. He was behind the other spectators, almost hiding. He had a grey scarf wrapped around his neck and mouth, and wore a black beanie hat. I smiled at Trevor, but when he saw me, he looked away.

Finally, our team started to improve. Within five minutes, Albie had scored. As the second half went on, we were the better side. We pressed the Southfield players and kept winning the ball from them. Ten minutes before the end, I passed the ball between two Southfield defenders. Thiágo ran onto the pass. Calmly, he slotted the ball past their keeper. 2–2!

Our families went wild – cheering and shouting for us. I fist-bumped my best friend.

"One more to win!" said Thiágo. "Just one more!"

From the re-start, he won the ball back and passed to me. I had four players in front of me. I dribbled past two and then passed to Albie. He was like a rabbit. Small and fast, and able to turn defenders inside out.

I saw what he was doing and sprinted to catch up. As I reached the penalty spot, Albie looked up and passed the ball behind two Southfield players. It was timed just right for me to run onto. I controlled it with one touch, turned past the last defender and smacked the ball into the net.

"COME ON!!!!!!!" I heard Byron yelling as I turned to celebrate the winning goal.

Nana-ji was grinning with pride. Behind him, I saw Trevor again. He gave me a little smile and a thumbs up, then turned and walked away. At the final whistle, our team jumped on each other to celebrate. It was a big win!

3

SUNDAY AT THE GURDWARA

The next morning, we went to the local Sikh temple, which is called a *gurdwara*. The building was once a small school. Upstairs, there is a long, wide prayer room, and downstairs, there's a community centre, kitchen and dining hall.

I go most Sundays, and I help serve food in the kitchen after the busy prayer service. Gurdwaras serve food for free, to anyone who wants it. Sikhs call this *langar*. It is part of our duty to help others, and I enjoy doing it.

By mid-afternoon, things had grown quiet at the gurdwara, so I went to find my mum. She was sitting at a table with several people we saw regularly there on a Sunday. They were eating some Punjabi food – all vegetarian, because most Sikhs don't eat meat. After working in the kitchen, my clothes reeked of cooked onions and spices. But I didn't mind.

Mum handed me a leaflet. "We're setting up a mobile food bank," she told me. "What do you think?"

The leaflet showed a white van with a hatch on one side. It was like the ones you see selling food on roadsides sometimes.

"It's cool," I told her. "Whose van is it?"

"Mine," said Mum. "At least it will be. It arrives tomorrow."

The logo on the van read "Wigby Community Meals Project".

"It's part of my new role," said Mum.

She worked across our community, with youth centres and libraries and various groups.

"We run the food bank already," said Mum. "Now, we want to make it mobile too, with hot meals."

"Where will the food come from?" I asked.

"The gurdwara on some days," said Mum.

"We're taking langar on the road?" I added.

"Yep," replied Mum. "Well, as long as the gurdwara committee allow us to. We'll need to use the kitchen here to cook the food. Then we can put it in trays and take it around in the van."

The committee is a group of volunteers who help to run the gurdwara. Nana-ji is one of them.

"So, people like us will donate the ingredients," Mum continued. "And we can help many more people."

I nodded, although I didn't really understand. Were there lots of hungry people in our community?

★

Mrs Richardson also talked about hungry people on Monday morning. I was sitting with Thiágo at the table closest to the front of the classroom. Maisie and Bella sat with us.

"Do you remember how we gathered Harvest donations for the food bank, Year 6?" said Mrs Richardson.

We all nodded.

"Well, with Christmas coming soon, we thought we'd try to help the food bank again.

We're going to ask you to donate old toys and clothes and other things."

"For a jumble sale?" asked Maisie.

"Exactly," said Mrs Richardson. "The money we raise will go to the food bank. We'll also collect food donations again too."

I put my hand up.

"Yes, Bobby?" Mrs Richardson said.

"My mum runs the food bank at the community centre," I told her.

"Really?" Mrs Richardson replied. "That's great. I think I might have a chat with your mum."

Maisie leaned towards me. "It's really cool your mum does that," she said.

"Yeah, I suppose it is," I replied.

"It definitely is," Maisie told me. "Your mum must be cooler than an ice-skating penguin!"

★

Later that evening, I was in the kitchen looking at quotes from Guru Nanak, the founder of

Sikhism, just out of interest. There was one that stood out, and I didn't know what it meant.

Nana-ji saw my confusion as he made tea in his City mug, while wearing an old City shirt. "What's up, kid?" he asked me.

"I don't understand this quote from Guru-ji," I replied.

I read it aloud: "*Whatever kind of seed is sown in a field, prepared in due season, a plant of that same kind, marked with the peculiar qualities of the seed, springs up in it ...*"

Nana-ji smiled. "Think of the seed as love," he explained. "If you plant a seed of love, then love will grow. If you plant a seed of hate, then hate will grow."

I nodded as the meaning became clearer.

"So, if I plant a seed of kindness, kindness grows?" I asked.

"Exactly," he said. "We get back what we give out. Being kind will create more kindness in the world."

"I love it," I replied.

I took a screenshot of the quote and saved it to my laptop.

4

WIGBY COMMUNITY MEALS

One of the most important things in Sikhism is
sewa, which means selfless service. It's the idea
of helping other people, no matter who they are
or where they come from, and not expecting
anything in return. It's something I've always
been taught, and I try to do it whenever I can.
It shows that Sikhs believe in everyone being
equal and try to live unselfish lives. Mum says
it allows us to understand others too. Empathy,
she calls it.

So I was happy to help Mum when the van
was ready a week later and she asked me if
I'd like to join in. I enjoy spending time with

Mum, but also her project was about spreading kindness, and I wanted to be part of that.

After school on Thursday, Mum drove us to the gurdwara. Several large pans of food were waiting for us. Brown lentil dal, spinach and potatoes, plain yoghurt, freshly fried pakoras, a simple salad of onions, tomatoes and cucumber. There was also a massive pot of rice pudding spiced with cinnamon and cardamom – my favourite. Next to these was a massive pile of steaming hot *roti* – the Punjabi word for chapattis, which are flatbreads.

Mum gave me a stack of foil cartons and cardboard lids. "Your job is to fill these with *saag aloo*," she told me.

Saag aloo is a dish made of spinach and potatoes. With a serving ladle, Mum showed me how to make portions that were the right size. Around us, other volunteers were helping too, including Nana-ji.

"Cover each carton with a lid and set them aside," Mum added.

"Where are they going?" I asked.

"We're taking them to people across Wigby," she told me.

"Me too?"

"If you want to come along," said Mum. "We have over forty people to deliver to. Nana-ji is helping me."

An hour later, we had packed half the food into Mum's new van. The rest of the deliveries were being made by someone else on Mum's team.

"Room for a small one?" Nana-ji joked, coming to the door of the van. He wore a pale blue turban and had oiled his beard so that it was neater than usual.

"Smelly one, you mean," I said.

"Cheeky little plop!" Nana-ji said.

"Dad!" replied Mum.

"Oh, get a sense of humour!" he told her.

Mum groaned, started the van and drove out of the gurdwara car park. I was so proud of her and what she was doing. And I was excited to be involved.

We worked fast. Mum drove to each address, and after she parked, I helped Nana-ji deliver the food. There were six cartons for each address, and roti in a foil wrap, all in a brown paper bag.

Everyone we met was happy to see us, and I chatted with a few different people. They were young and old, and of all different backgrounds. I was sad to see how many people needed food, but I was grateful that I could help. Nana-ji called it an honour and a privilege, and I agreed with him.

Soon, we had completed most of the deliveries. Mum parked outside some flats close to the park and community centre.

"We're delivering to six people here," she said. "Then we can go home. You must be tired, kid."

"I'm OK," I told her, but I *was* getting a bit weary. I just didn't want to admit it.

I gathered three bags, and Nana-ji took the other three. But we stayed together. As a child, I wasn't allowed to deliver food alone. Mum stayed in the van.

The block of flats had two floors, so we delivered to the four people upstairs first, then headed down. At the last flat, I knocked, and Trevor opened the door. He looked surprised to see me.

"Your delivery, Mr Ambrose," said Nana-ji. He looked in the bag. "Oh, we forgot the roti."

"I can get them," I told him.

"No, I'll go," Nana-ji replied. "The van is only just outside, and I can see you through the main door. I won't be long."

I smiled at Trevor and handed him his bag.

"Smells good," he told me.

"It does," I replied. "It's making me hungry."

Trevor went back into his small flat and put the bag down. I could hear a reggae song playing and see into his lounge.

"Do you live alone?" I asked when he returned.

"Yes," Trevor said. "Ever since my wife passed."

"I'm sorry to hear that," I told him. "My nana-ji lost his wife too."

Trevor looked puzzled, so I explained, "That's my grandad," I said. "The man who is with me."

"That's the Punjabi word for grandad then?" he asked.

"One of them, yes," I replied.

Trevor looked away, as if there was something interesting behind me. His expression was glum.

"My wife was all I had left," he whispered. "There's nothing worth going out for now."

"Apart from watching us play football?" I said.

"I do enjoy that sometimes," he told me. "That coach of yours – he knows his stuff."

"Byron," I said. "Our coach's name is Byron Dixon. He's a great coach. Nana-ji enjoys watching us play too, and he used to love playing football when he was younger."

"I remember you telling me," said Trevor. "At the food bank."

"Oh, yeah," I replied. "Nana-ji was one of the first Asians to watch City play."

"Really?" Trevor replied.

"He always tells me stories about those days," I continued. "Maybe you should speak to him at a game some time?"

"Maybe," said Trevor. "But really there's no use talking about the old days, son. Can't bring them back. And nothing will bring back playing football."

Nana-ji returned with the roti and handed the foil wrap to Trevor. "Sorry about that. It's been a busy night," he said. Then Nana-ji stopped and listened. "Is that song in the background by Dennis Brown?"

Trevor's eyes widened, and he smiled. "Yeah, man," he said. "It's called—"

"'Here I Come'," Nana-ji replied. "I have it."

"You know reggae?" asked Trevor.

"I love it," said Nana-ji. "Was the soundtrack to my youth."

"Yeah?" replied Trevor. "Me too!"

They stood and smiled at each other for a moment. Nana-ji was even tapping his right foot to the song.

"Anyway," said Trevor, "goodnight, young man, and goodnight, Nana-ji."

"I'm Bobby," I reminded him. I was surprised and amused that Trevor had used the Punjabi word for grandad.

"Bobby," he repeated. "Good name for a footballer, that. You go home now and get your rest. It's a school night."

"Goodnight, Mr Ambrose," I replied.

I went home and thought about the Guru Nanak quote as I tried to sleep. We had planted many seeds that evening. I wondered how many would grow.

5

AN EXCITING ASSEMBLY

Nana-ji searched in the attic later that week, and on Sunday night he sat on my bed, looking at some old photographs.

"This is me at twenty years old," he said. "I haven't seen these in years!"

He looked totally different. No turban or beard, and long, curly brown hair. He was standing with five other men, all dressed in a similar way. They wore striped jumpers under tracksuit tops, and wide-legged trousers with chunky Adidas trainers. One of them had a checked scarf wrapped around his neck and over his mouth. Nana-ji was the only Asian one.

"I think that was when City played
Manchester United at home," Nana-ji told me.
"We lost, but it was a fun match."

"Did you go to all the games?" I asked.

"Most of them," he said.

Nana-ji showed me another photograph. This time, he was outside a pub. He was standing next to his best friend, Danny. Danny often came over to see Nana-ji, and I knew him well.

"Trevor must be about your age," I told him.

"Probably," he replied. "What's his surname again? Maybe I knew him back in the day."

"Ambrose," I said.

Nana-ji thought for a minute, scratching his white beard. "Trevor Ambrose," he said. "I can't remember anyone I knew personally, but ..."

"But what?"

"The name feels familiar," Nana-ji replied. "But I can't think why."

"You could ask him?" I added.

"Ask him about what?"

"Whether you knew him back when you had hair," I said.

"You really are annoying," Nana-ji replied. "Has anyone ever told you that?"

"Yeah, you," I reminded him. "Like, ten times a day since I was a toddler ..."

Nana-ji shook his head.

"Nah," he continued, "you were cute as a toddler. Then something flipped, and now you stink like a baboon and you're annoying."

"I don't smell as bad as you," I joked back.

"Years of practice, son," he replied. "I've got experience."

"And a shiny head," I added. Then I asked, "Have you really got that song Trevor was playing?"

"Yeah, it's in my room."

Nana-ji went and got the record, which he called a seven inch. He handed it to me.

"See?"

"You could get to know him better," I suggested. "Talk about reggae and football, and the old days before cars and electricity ..."

He grinned and said, "You like him, don't you?"

"He seems nice," I replied. "I think he's lonely because his wife passed away. And sad because he can't play football any more."

"Sounds like we have a few things in common then," said Nana-ji.

"He'd probably enjoy the company," I added. "You too."

"Yeah," said Nana-ji. "Maybe ..."

★

The next morning, Mrs Richardson took assembly. Our school is old and small, built in 1855. The building is long and narrow, with three floors. The hall is on the ground floor, and we use it for dinner-time too. We only have about thirty children in each school year and sit in year groups for assemblies. There's the youngest at the front and the oldest at the back. My teacher called for quiet before speaking.

"So," Mrs Richardson said, "with Christmas here soon, I thought I'd outline what we'll be doing to celebrate."

Some of the children cheered.

"Settle down now," said Mrs Richardson with a smile.

"Yes, Miss!" we all replied.

"So, decorations day is next Friday. We'll be asking parents to join us in the classrooms to help."

Most of the children began to whisper excitedly.

"Four Year 6 pupils will help set up and decorate both Christmas trees," Mrs Richardson went on. "There will be one in the foyer, and one here in the hall. Those children are Bella, Thiágo, Maisie and Bobby."

"Yes!" Maisie and Bella shouted together.

"Calm down, girls," said Mrs Richardson. "We'll also have a post box for Christmas cards and decorate the corridors and foyer. And now, for my favourite part, the Christmas Fundraising Fair."

There were more cheers and smiles now. We all loved the Christmas Fair.

"Settle down," she said again after a moment. "So, we are collecting donations of toys, games, clothes, small household items, gifts – whatever you can give for a jumble sale. We'll also have raffle prizes. And we'll be supporting Wigby Community Meals Project in their amazing work."

Maisie nudged me in the side. "That's your mum's project!" she said.

"Yeah," I whispered.

Maisie grinned at me before turning back to Bella. "I want to do his mum's job when I'm older," she said.

"Me too," replied Bella, "but I want to work with koala bears too. And climb mountains."

"*Oooh*, koala bears," said Maisie, and they both began to giggle. They did that a lot.

"Remember what I always say, children," Mrs Richardson added. "The spirit of Christmas isn't about receiving gifts. It's about sharing and kindness and looking after each other. Community and family and friends. Those we already know and those we have yet to meet."

After assembly, Mrs Richardson told me to wait behind. "I've had an idea," she told me. "I want to get your local football team involved with the Christmas Fair too – open it up to the local community. Do you think Byron would join in?"

"I'm sure he'd love it!" I said. "I'll ask him tomorrow, Miss – we have a game then."

"Thank you, Bobby," said Mrs Richardson. "I do love the run-up to Christmas. So exciting!"

"Me too, Miss!" I said.

6

SOWING A SEED OF KINDNESS

Wigby FC Juniors didn't often play a midweek game. But a severe storm had meant that we'd missed a game from the schedule and needed to play that fixture before Christmas. It was a bad game for us – a goalless draw against Northfield Juniors, who were bottom of our league.

We had expected to win, which was part of the problem. We were so confident, we didn't play as a team. We were still top of the league, but Southfield would get closer if they won their next game.

Afterwards, I told Byron about my teacher's idea.

"Mrs Richardson can call me any time," he said. "Linking the football club with the school and the food bank is a brilliant idea."

"Thanks, Coach!" I said. "She'll be really pleased."

"I know," he said with a wink. "Mrs Richardson used to teach me years ago, when she first started at Wigby."

"No way – that's like decades ago!"

Byron laughed. "I'm not *that* old," he replied.

"Yeah, you can still play football," I said. "Nana-ji would love to play, but he says his bones hurt and his knee is ruined. Mr Ambrose is the same. He loves football, but he can't run now."

"Mr Ambrose?" Byron asked.

"Yeah," I said. "The old man who watches us play sometimes. Trevor Ambrose."

"Oh, yeah," Byron replied. "That name seems familiar ..."

"He's lonely too," I added. "I want to help him."

"He should try walking football," Byron suggested. "Your nana-ji too."

"Walking football?" I asked. "What's that?"

Byron grinned. "Exactly what it says," he told me. "You don't run; you walk. It's like five-a-side but at a slow pace. It's very popular with older people."

"Is there a club they can join?" I asked.

"Not around here," said Byron. We'd reached the car park, where Mum was waiting. "But if people are interested, they could set up a game. It's very easy to do."

"What's easy to do?" asked Mum as she hugged Byron.

She and Byron had gone to school together and were close friends.

"We were talking about a walking football game for older people," said Byron. "Nana-ji and Mr Ambrose miss playing football. I think Bobby is on a mission to help them."

Mum smiled at me. "You like Trevor, don't you?" she said. It was something Nana-ji had also said.

Thing is, I did like Trevor – he was a cool old dude, like Nana-ji. I hated that he felt so lonely and sat home on his own most of the time. Giving people food when they needed it was really important. But so was giving them something to look forward to. It was a seed of kindness that I was determined to sow.

"Trevor is nice," I said. "I think he should make friends with Nana-ji. They're about the same age, I think. And they both lost their wives and they both love reggae, so ..."

I stopped to take a breath, and Mum and Byron both grinned.

"Easy now," said Byron.

"It's the kind thing to do," I said. "Helping people will make me a better Sikh."

"Well, you can't force them to be friends," said Mum. "But maybe you should speak to Nana-ji about setting up a walking football game?"

"I'm gonna do that," I replied.

★

I was so excited about the idea that I explained it to Nana-ji that night.

"Sounds like fun," said Nana-ji. "I wonder if we can get something organised?"

"You could call Byron," I told him. "Like, now. I'm sure he would help us."

Nana-ji smiled. "You're always in a rush," he said. "It can wait."

"Please?" I begged. "Then you can make friends with Trevor, and you can play the game before Christmas. It would be awesome. Like a special Christmas present for older people in the community."

"You mean a present for Trevor," replied Nana-ji with a smile.

"You too," I told him. "When was the last time *you* played football?"

Nana-ji sighed. "That was a long time ago," he told me.

"I know you miss it," I replied.

"Yes, I do," he admitted.

"*Pleeeeaaassse?*" I begged again.

Nana-ji nodded. "I know a few old lads who'd love a game," he said. "Go ask your mum for Byron's phone number. We'll have a chat."

Ten minutes later, I felt nervous as I sat listening to Nana-ji's conversation with my football coach. I really wanted the game to happen.

As their conversation ended, Nana-ji was grinning. "Byron's even more excited than you," he told me. "He said he knows loads of older folk who miss playing. He wants to organise a game for the Christmas Fair."

"But they can't play at my school," I replied. "We don't have a football pitch."

"Not at your school," said Nana-ji. "The fair is taking place at the community centre. Ask your mum – she's organised it with Mrs Richardson and the school."

I suddenly remembered what Mrs Richardson had said about speaking to Mum. I'd been so excited about the walking football game that I'd forgotten.

"Wow!" I said. "That's going to be epic!"

"Yes," said Nana-ji. "It is. I'd better get my old trainers out then!"

He gave me a bear-hug. "You're a good kid, Bobby," Nana-ji told me. "Whiffy, sure, but kind too."

"I told you before," I replied, "I'm never as smelly as you."

"Ah, yes," said Nana-ji, "but I've had more years to perfect my pong!"

7

PERSEVERE!

The following Wednesday, it was even colder, and football practice was hard. But I had other things on my mind. Well, one thing – the walking football game. I wanted to tell Trevor all about it and hoped he'd be at the food bank at the community centre.

After practice, I rushed into the community centre. I saw Trevor sitting at a table with two other men and smiled to myself. They were playing cards and drinking tea. The food bank was running but very quiet. I found Mum washing plates at the sink.

"How was football practice?" she asked.

"Penguin-level cold," I replied.

"*That* bad, kid?" Mum said.

I touched her cheek with my left hand.

"Bobby!" she shouted.

"See?" I said. "Colder than Rudolph's hooves."

She laughed.

"Byron is definitely organising the walking football game," I told her. "He told me today. Nana-ji is playing too!"

"That's great news," Mum replied. "Nana-ji will love that. I mean, he'll never stop talking about it afterwards, but he'll have fun ..."

"He'll just exaggerate about how well he played," I said. "I'll tell Trevor now. He's playing cards in the hall."

"Keeping warm with the others," said Mum. "But we need to close soon."

"I won't be long," I said.

Trevor seemed pleased to see me. "Bobby!" he said.

"Sorry to interrupt," I replied.

"No, no," said Trevor. "I was just about to go home anyway. Is there something on your mind?"

I nodded. Trevor stood and put on his grey coat and black beanie hat, then said goodbye to the others. I waited until he was ready to leave.

"I had an idea," I told him.

"What's that?" Trevor asked.

"About the football," I explained.

He sighed. "I told you, son," he said, "I can't play any more. Can't run."

"What if you could play walking football?"

"What?" Trevor frowned.

"It's like five-a-side but slower," I explained. "You just walk."

"Walk and play?" he said. "Sounds strange."

"Byron and Nana-ji are organising a game to be played during the school Christmas Fair. Nana-ji is going to take part too. It'll be fun."

I told Trevor when the fair was happening. He looked away, and his expression changed. He seemed glum again.

"I can't," he told me. "I just ..."

He looked at me with watery eyes. "I know you mean well, Bobby," Trevor said softly, "but some things are best left behind."

"I don't understand," I said.

Trevor shrugged. "I have to go," he replied. "See you around, kid."

I don't know what I was expecting, but I felt as sad as Trevor looked. Why wasn't he more excited? Had I said something wrong?

★

I was still sad at school the next day. Maisie and Bella noticed and tried their best to cheer me up.

"We could do the 'Walk Like an Egyptian' dance?" Maisie offered. The dance was from an old song that she'd listened to with her dad. The dance was funny, but I wasn't in the mood. I was thinking about Trevor and why he had reacted to the walking football game like that.

"Or 'Walk Like a Giraffe Wearing High Heels'?" Bella added.

"That's OK," I replied. "I'll be fine soon."

"Soon is not now," said Maisie. "And we can't have you feeling unhappy. We're your friends, and it's our job to make you happy."

"Your job," Bella told her. "I like making boys cry."

Bella giggled at her own silly joke and then walked off to annoy a boy called Etienne. Maisie offered me a purple eraser shaped like a berry.

"You can have this if you smile," she said. "It even smells like a blackberry."

"I'm good," I replied.

Maisie sat next to me. "Are you sure you're OK?" she asked.

I shrugged. "There's this man who comes to my football practice sometimes," I told her.

"He's lonely, and he doesn't have much money. I wanted to help him, but he didn't like my idea."

I explained about the walking football game Byron was setting up.

"That sounds awesome," Maisie said. "But you can't make him play."

"That's what Mum said," I replied.

"But you shouldn't give up either," Maisie added. "You can try again, like Mrs Richardson always tells us. Persevere, young man! Persevere!"

Mrs Richardson gave us a stern look, and Maisie lowered her voice to a whisper.

"Try again," she suggested.

"Thanks," I replied. "I will."

"And, Bobby?" Maisie added.

"Yeah?"

"Don't tell the other boys I was nice to you," she said.

Maisie grinned and then joined Bella.

8

A MYSTERY

But I didn't get the chance to try again with
Trevor, as he disappeared for the whole week.
He didn't show up at the community centre
and missed our last football practice before
Christmas too.

"Did Trevor ask for a food delivery?" I asked
Mum the day before the Christmas Fair.

"You know I can't share private details
about people, Bobby," she replied.

"But what if something bad has happened
to him?"

"I'm sure he's fine," Mum said.

The entire community was excited about the Christmas Fair. Byron told me that twenty-four people had signed up for walking football too. One more person would make five teams for five-a-side. I was praying that extra person would be Trevor.

"Maybe he'll see the posters for the fair and that will remind him?" I said to Mum.

Mum shrugged. She was busy on her laptop, working, so I went to watch telly. A few minutes later, Nana-ji walked into the house with Byron. Nana-ji was holding an old football-sticker album.

"Bobby!" Nana-ji said excitedly. "I've remembered!"

I wondered what he meant and why Byron was with him. "Remembered what, Nana-ji?" I asked.

Both he and Byron grinned.

"He's called Trevor Ambrose, right?" said Byron.

"Yes, Coach," I replied. "Why?"

"And I said the name sounded familiar?" Nana-ji added.

I nodded.

"I realised who Trevor actually is," Byron said.

"I don't understand," I told them. "Is he a spy or something weird like that?"

"No," said Byron. "But Trevor was a professional footballer once. He played in an FA Cup final and won a medal with United."

"Huh?" I said, shocked.

"Here he is!" Nana-ji exclaimed. "Look!"

He opened the old album and tapped a sticker.

"Trevor Ambrose," Nana-ji said. "I should have known!"

I looked at the sticker. It showed a smiling young man with afro hair in a United shirt. Nana-ji and Byron were right. It was Trevor!

"Wow!" I said. "That's awesome!" But then I frowned. "What happened to him?"

Byron shrugged. "That's the mystery," he replied. "Trevor scored thirty-six goals in forty games. He was supposed to be a superstar player."

"But then he just disappeared," said Nana-ji. "I think I remember him having some troubles, and he got dropped from the team. The newspapers said he moved to Canada. Then they forgot about him."

"I can't believe I didn't recognise him," Byron said.

"Doesn't matter," I told them. "He won't play anyway. And I haven't seen him for over a week."

"Maybe *we* should speak to him," said Nana-ji. "We have to try."

"We?" I asked.

Nana-ji grinned. "It was your idea, Bobby," he replied. "You and I should go."

"When?" I asked.

Byron and Nana-ji looked at each other.

"There's no time like the present," said Byron. "But it's freezing. I'll give you a lift."

Byron dropped us off, and I stood at Trevor's door and knocked twice. When he didn't answer, I knocked again. Then I heard him grumbling and complaining inside.

"I'm nervous," I said.

Nana-ji smiled. "Don't worry," he said. "He can only say no, Bobby."

Trevor opened the door and stared at us for a moment. He looked tired.

"Bobby?" he said at last.

"Hello," I replied.

Trevor looked at Nana-ji. "I don't understand," he said. "What's going on?"

Nana-ji nudged me. I opened my bag and took out the football-sticker album.

"I know who you really are," I said.

I showed Trevor his sticker. His expression softened, and I thought he was going to cry.

Then he smiled sadly. "I suppose you'd better come in," he said.

Trevor led us into the living room. It was small and tidy, with a sofa and a small table. An armchair faced the window, with a view of the park and the community centre. I wondered if he often sat there, watching the world pass him by.

"Have a seat," Trevor said.

Opposite the window was an old music system with big speakers. A load of vinyl records were piled up beside it.

"Reggae records," said Nana-ji as he sat down.

Trevor smiled. "I used to have loads more," he said.

Nana-ji got up and looked through the records.

"These must be very rare now," he said to Trevor.

"Yeah, man," Trevor replied. "Some of those tunes are impossible to get today."

"I sold most of mine," Nana-ji told him. "I regret it now."

Trevor turned his armchair towards us and sat down too. "So," he said. "What can I do for you?"

I opened the sticker album. "Why didn't you tell me that you were a professional football player?" I asked.

"I didn't want to," said Trevor. "Those days feel like a different life. I didn't want to make a fuss."

"But you were a superstar," I replied.

"For a short time, maybe," Trevor said. "But things got difficult, and I had to move on."

I nodded and looked at his sticker again. "What happened?" I asked.

Trevor looked at Nana-ji, then back at me. "Life," he said. "I had some problems dealing with the fame. Got myself into trouble. The team manager dumped me."

"Is that why you moved to Canada?" asked Nana-ji.

"Yeah," said Trevor. "I had to leave. Had to get away from everything. I met my wife, Denise, in Canada. I only came back because she passed on."

Trevor nodded to a framed photograph on the windowsill. It showed Trevor and a happy, smiling woman wearing a T-shirt that said "Vancouver State".

"I still talk to her sometimes," he revealed. "When I sit looking out at the park."

"I'm sorry for your loss," said Nana-ji. "I know how hard it is."

"Bobby told me you also lost your wife," said Trevor.

"Yes, I miss her too," Nana-ji replied. "But I'm lucky to have Bobby and his mum."

"Denise and I never had kids," Trevor told him.

"Will you come and play walking football tomorrow?" I asked.

"I told you," said Trevor. "I'm not sure I want to."

"Will you think about it?" I added.

Trevor stood and looked at his records. "You're very direct, son," he said. "Tell me why you're so interested."

I thought about what to say. Meanwhile, Trevor turned on his stereo and put a record on his turntable.

"This is Robert Marley," he said. "Before he became Bob Marley. His first ever tune – the original record. My dad gave it to me."

I heard the record crackling and hissing as it started to play. Then the song began.

"Wow – I remember hearing this years ago!" said Nana-ji.

Trevor looked at me.

"I know I'm only young," I told him. "But I was taught to care about other human beings. A seed of kindness helps kindness to grow and spread. You're part of our community, Mr Ambrose, and we should look after each other. That's what my religion teaches me."

Trevor listened and then smiled. "You're a good kid," he told me.

"I try to be," I replied.

"I can't promise anything, Bobby," he said. "But I'll think about it."

9

SIGN ME UP!

The Christmas Fair was busy despite the cold weather. It opened with our whole school singing carols in the community centre. Then the jumble sale and raffle started. Outside, Byron ran a penalty shootout. Bella and Maisie were first in line, and they kept going back.

"We're better than the boys!" Maisie said to me and Thiágo.

"In your dreams," Thiágo told her.

"Let's have a challenge then," said Bella. "Boys versus girls!"

Byron gave us the ball. "Five penalties for each team," he said, and took up his position in goal.

I scored first, and then Bella scored too. But as Thiágo took our second penalty, Maisie nudged him, and he missed.

"Maisie!" Thiágo shouted.

"Wasn't me," she replied. "It was the invisible penguin."

"Yeah," said Bella. "It was a V.I.P."

"Huh?" I asked.

"A Very Invisible Penguin!" Maisie and Bella said at the same time.

"There's no invisible penguin!" said Thiágo.

Bella looked at me and frowned. "That's the problem with boys," she said. "They have no imagination."

The girls won the penalty shootout, and they were teasing us so badly that Thiágo went to find his mum and sisters.

"Mardy bum!" said Maisie.

Nana-ji was serving hot samosas and chickpea curry at a stall. The gurdwara had donated the food, and it was very popular. I saw Maisie's dad chatting to Bella's mum as they ate.

"How's it going?" I asked Nana-ji.

"Brilliant!" he said. "People are loving the food! Have a samosa."

I shook my head. "Maybe later," I said. "It's almost time for the walking football game."

"I'd better get my trainers on then," Nana-ji replied. "Can't wait!"

I looked across the park, towards Trevor's flat. Would he come? I wondered.

Byron finished the penalty shootouts and asked us to help with the walking football. Bella, Maisie and I marked out a small pitch using cones. Then Byron set up a goal at each end.

"We've got twenty-four people," Byron said. "So there will be four teams of five, with four subs."

"Trevor still might turn up," I said. But I was hoping, rather than certain.

"Fingers crossed," said Byron.

The first game was strange, because of the slow pace. It was odd watching people walk to kick the football. But when Nana-ji and his team began their game next, I was really excited. And when Nana-ji scored, I jumped up and down with joy.

"Go on, Nana-ji!" I heard from behind me. "Get in, Mr Singh!"

I turned to find Trevor smiling at me. He was wearing a black tracksuit under his coat, and old blue trainers.

"You came!" I said excitedly.

"Couldn't let you down, could I?" Trevor said.

My football coach was even more excited than me. "Mr Ambrose," Byron said, grinning and shaking his hand. "It's an honour. A real honour!"

Trevor looked embarrassed, but he kept on smiling. "Can I join a team?" he asked.

"Yes, of course!" said Byron.

Trevor began the next game, and he was amazing. His control of the ball was brilliant, despite only walking. It seemed stuck to his foot. And then Trevor scored a screamer with his left foot.

Me and Byron whooped with joy, and Trevor grinned at us.

When he came off the pitch, I ran up to him. "Did you have fun?" I asked.

Trevor smiled but had tears in his eyes. "That was ..." he began, then wiped his eyes. "Thank you, Bobby. I don't know what to say but thank you!"

As Nana-ji and Byron joined us, I gave Trevor a big hug. "You're welcome," I said. "Very welcome."

"I could get used to this walking football," said Trevor.

"Good," said Byron. "Because I'm going to turn it into a weekly thing. You up for it, Mr Ambrose?"

Trevor winked at him. "Sign me up!" he said. "But next time, remind me to wear my hat. It's freezing!"

★

The rest of the Christmas Fair went just as well. At the end, Mum invited Trevor home for dinner. He spent the evening telling us old stories and laughing with Nana-ji. When it was time for Trevor to leave, I felt a bit sad.

"Can Trevor come over for Christmas Day?" I asked Mum.

She looked at Trevor, and Nana-ji, who was nodding so hard I thought his head might come off.

"We do a vegetarian Christmas," Mum said. "But you're more than welcome to join us."

"*If* you bring some reggae records for us to play," said Nana-ji.

"You can come even if you don't," I added.

Trevor looked at me and smiled warmly. "I'd like that," he said. "I'd like that very much."